*Tilly's Pony Tails*

# Buttons
## the naughty pony

# Tilly's Pony Tails
# Buttons
## the naughty pony

## Pippa Funnell

Illustrated by Jennifer Miles

Orion
Children's Books

First published in Great Britain in 2011
by Orion Children's Books
This new edition published in 2013
a division of the Orion Publishing Group Ltd
Orion House
5 Upper St Martin's Lane
London WC2H 9EA
An Hachette UK Company

5 7 9 10 8 6 4

Text copyright © Pippa Funnell MBE 2011, 2012
Illustrations copyright © Jennifer Miles 2011

ISBN 978 1 4440 0260 7

Printed and bound by CPI Group
(UK) Ltd, Croydon, CR0 4YY

www.orionbooks.co.uk
www.tillysponytails.co.uk

*For Isabel Saywell,*
*to encourage her reading*

# Hello!

When I was little, I, like Tilly, was absolutely crazy about horses and ponies. All my books, pictures and toys had something to do with my four-legged friends.

I was lucky because a great friend of my mother's lent us a little woolly pony called Pepsi. He lived in the field at my best friend's house. I loved spending as much time as possible with him, but hated having to scrape all the mud off his shaggy winter coat. I used to lie in bed at night longing for the day I'd be able to have a smart horse all clipped and snuggled up in a stable with nice warm rugs.

My birthday treat every year was to go to The Horse of the Year Show, and

I remember going to Badminton and Burghley as a child. It was seeing top riders at these famous venues that gave me the inspiration to follow my dreams.

Now I've had the opportunity to ride some wonderful horses, all of whom have a special place in my heart. It's thanks to them that I have achieved my dreams and won so many competitions at the highest level. I still ride all day, every day, live, sleep and breathe horses and I love every minute of it.

Many of you will not be as used to horses as I am, so I have tried to include some of what I have learned in these books. At the back is a glossary so you can look up any unfamiliar words.

I hope you will enjoy reading the books in my series *Tilly's Pony Tails*, as much as I have enjoyed creating a girl who, like me, follows her passions. I hope that Tilly will inspire many readers to follow their dreams.

Love

# One

Tilly Redbrow was busy cleaning tack at Silver Shoe Farm. She'd been scrubbing and polishing in the tack room all morning. It was early July and outside the sun was shining, but she didn't let this put her off. Magic Spirit's saddle looked as good as new. Tilly smiled to herself, admired her effort and breathed the scent of saddle oil – it was one of her favourite smells. It was just as well, because Angela insisted that all the bridles and saddles used every day were properly cleaned and looked after. The better tack was cared for, the longer it would last.

When she had finished, Tilly tipped the soapy water down the sink, put the saddle oil and cloth into a bucket, and popped everything into the cupboard where it belonged. She hung up the clean halter, bridle and girth, and put the saddle on its rack.

Just then Angela, Silver Shoe's owner popped her head around the door.

'Hi, Tilly. I've been looking for you. We've got a new arrival coming this afternoon – a little pony called Buttons. His owners have warned that he can be quite naughty. You were so useful when it came to getting Cynthia and Parkview Pickle settled, I thought maybe you could give me a hand today?'

'Definitely,' said Tilly, feeling pleased. It was an honour to be asked to help by someone as experienced as Angela. 'What do you want me to do?'

'It would be great if you could be around when the trailer arrives. Watch out for the way Buttons responds to his owners when they lead him out, see if you notice anything. It's a mum and son. The boy is about your age. His name's Tim. Could you show him around and help him make friends?'

'Sure,' said Tilly. 'Tim and Buttons. I'll remember that.'

'Thanks. I knew I could count on you.'

As Angela walked away, Tilly wondered about the new arrivals. Was it a problem pony or problem owners? She knew that sometimes a horse's behaviour was due to the way it was treated. She was intrigued. She couldn't wait to meet them.

The trailer arrived just after lunch. Tilly and Angela were waiting in the yard.

'Hello!'

'Hi,' said Angela. 'I'm Angela. We spoke on the phone. Welcome to Silver Shoe. How was your journey?'

'Fine, thanks. Although I'm not sure what Buttons will be like when we get him out,' said Tim's mum.

She was small with a blonde ponytail. Tim looked just like her, with tufty blonde hair and freckles. They both had tanned skin, which suggested they spent a lot of time outdoors.

'Hi,' said Tim. He smiled at Tilly. She smiled back.

'This is Tilly,' said Angela. 'She's going to show you around.'

'Nice to meet you.'

'I'll get Buttons,' said Tim's mum. She raised an eyebrow. 'Tim, you'd better give me a hand.'

Tim went in through the jockey door of the trailer, while his mum lowered the ramp. There was quiet for a moment as they disappeared inside. Tilly watched with anticipation. She heard a shuffling of hooves and lots of encouraging talk, but no sign of Buttons.

Tilly and Angela crept closer. Eventually Buttons appeared, led by Tim's mum. He was small, with a delicate frame and a sweet face, but he was putting up a fierce resistance. He didn't seem to want to move. He kept tossing his head and stamping his front hoof.

Tilly thought Tim and his mum seemed confident around Buttons, so it

couldn't be their nerves that were affecting him. Maybe he just didn't like the trailer?

'Has he travelled much before?' said Angela, when Buttons was finally standing in the yard.

She came forward and stroked the little pony's nose. He had bright eyes and a dark tail and mane to complement his dappled grey coat. He seemed calmer now he was off the ramp, but he was still twitchy.

'A few times,' said Tim's mum. 'Being in the trailer is nothing new to him.'

'But we haven't had him that long,' said Tim. 'We inherited him from a farmer whose house we bought. He said he'd reared him from a foal.'

'Tim's always wanted his own horse or pony,' added Tim's mum. 'So it worked out perfectly for us to take Buttons off the farmer's hands, along with the land. It felt like a dream come true, didn't it?'

Tilly smiled. That had always been one of her dreams too.

Tim just rolled his eyes and muttered under his breath.

'I wish.'

His mum frowned.

'But as you know it hasn't been quite as smooth as we'd hoped, which is why we're here. Buttons is a lovely pony, and he and Tim seem to have bonded really well. Unfortunately neither of us has been able to do anything with him. When we try to catch him he makes a game of it. If we attempt to tack him up he nips us and tosses his head and makes it impossible.'

'I haven't managed to ride him once,' said Tim.

'We're baffled by it. Tim's had a horse on loan at another stables for a few years. We stopped doing that when we got Buttons, but it's been a nightmare!'

Angela shook her head.

'It all sounds very frustrating for you, but let's see what we can do. Tilly, why don't you take Tim and Buttons over to his stable and see if you can get him settled while I have a chat with his mum?'

Tilly watched with interest as Tim led Buttons towards the stable block. He was very calm and gave Buttons lots of attention – almost too much, Tilly thought. Every step of the way he made encouraging noises, tickled his ears, and told him what a good boy he was, but Buttons remained reluctant, stopping frequently and forcing Tim to work harder. He didn't seem worried about following commands or doing what he was told.

As they passed Magic's stable, Tilly reached up to pat him.

'This is Magic Spirit,' she said. 'This is my horse.'

Magic leaned over the stable door and gently nudged her cheek. She stroked his neck and kissed his nose.

'He's beautiful,' said Tim. 'It's obvious you two get on well. Do you do a lot of riding?'

'As much as possible,' said Tilly. 'There are some great countryside tracks round here. And recently we've done a lot of work on our jumping. We're getting better and better, aren't we, Magic?'

Magic nickered and pricked his ears. He rested his head on Tilly's shoulder.

'That makes me jealous,' said Tim. 'I'm desperate to start riding again. I just wish Buttons would let me. I love him but he's the pony from hell!'

'He can't be that bad,' said Tilly.

Tim shook his head. 'You'll see. What's it like here, anyway?'

'At Silver Shoe? Oh, it's the nicest stables in the area. Everyone's really friendly. Angela and Duncan – he's the head-boy – take good care of all the horses. Actually, Magic was a rescue horse. I found him abandoned at the side of a road. Angela picked him up and brought him to Silver Shoe and he's been here ever since.'

'Do you know a lot about horses?'

'A bit,' said Tilly, with a modest shrug.

'She's lying,' said a voice behind them. It was Tilly's friend, Mia.

'She's amazing with horses. Are you and Magic ready to go hacking, Tilly?'

'Hi, Mia. Meet Tim. And this is Buttons. I'll be ready in a bit – as soon as I've helped Tim get Buttons into his stable.'

'Sweet pony!' said Mia, as she patted Buttons on the nose.

'That's what everyone says,' Tim muttered. 'Don't be fooled.'

# Two

Buttons hesitated before going into his new stable. Luckily he reacted quickly to the clicking sound Tilly made, and she was glad he'd decided not to be stubborn – she was keen to go out hacking with Magic. Once he was inside, Buttons had a sniff in each corner then began to nibble contentedly at his hay-net.

'How did you know to make that

clicking noise when you did?' asked Tim.

'I don't know,' said Tilly. 'I guess I just sensed Buttons might complain about going into the stable, and clicking always seems to work when Magic is making a fuss.'

'He *always* fusses when he goes into the stable, I can't believe how he responded to your clicks. You really are amazing with horses.'

Tilly blushed. She didn't know what to say.

'He looks happy anyway,' said Tim, with a relieved shrug.

'I'm sure he will be,' said Tilly. ' I'd better go and meet Mia now, but I'll see you later.'

'See you.'

Tilly and Mia had a good ride along one of their favourite woodland tracks. They stayed out for nearly two hours and made the most of the fine weather. Arriving back at Silver Shoe, they saw Tim marching through the yard, looking very agitated.

'What's up?' said Tilly. 'How's it going with Buttons?'

'Not great. He was fine for a while but then we took him out to graze. Angela told me to put him in the small field where there was only one other horse. But he's caused trouble already.'

'What's he done?' said Mia.

'He chased the other horse down to the end of the field and gave her a nip on the back. We need to move him now but I just know he's going to be a nightmare to catch. I'm going to see if I can help.'

Reluctantly, Tim turned and continued down to the field. Tilly and Mia exchanged glances.

'Hold on,' Tilly called. 'We're coming too.'

Duncan and Angela were already at the small field with Buttons. Tilly watched carefully. Buttons would stand still for a second. Duncan would make an approach then Buttons would nod his head, snort and run away, his tail up in the air. It was like a game. He wasn't being threatening or dangerous, he just wasn't taking anyone seriously. If a pony could laugh, Tilly thought, Buttons would be laughing now.

'Is he always like this when you try to catch him?' she asked.

'Always.'

'Don't worry. Duncan will catch him eventually. He's worked with difficult horses before. In fact, my horse, Magic—'

'Yes?'

'Let's just say he can be a real pain when he wants to be.'

'Especially if your name's not Tilly Redbrow,' said Mia. 'She's the only person he'll behave for.'

'I'll see if they want a hand,' Tim said, climbing over the fence towards Duncan and Angela.

Mia turned to Tilly.

'It's a shame Jack Fisher isn't here,' she said. 'I bet he'd know what to do.'

Jack Fisher was Angela's dad. He'd
lived and worked at Silver Shoe Farm all
his life. He'd handed the responsibility of
managing it over to Angela, now that he
was older, but he still helped out and had
a wealth of knowledge about horse care,
training and riding. Tilly loved talking to
him and getting tips and ideas.

'You're right,' Tilly said. 'He'd know
exactly what to do. I wonder when he's
back from his holiday.'

'Tilly, could you run back to the yard and fetch a bucket of pony nuts?' called Duncan, spotting them at the fence. 'If I'd known he would be like this I would have come with one in the first place!'

'Sure,' said Tilly. 'Good idea!'

Eventually, with a little encouragement from the pony nuts, Buttons grew bored of his game and allowed Duncan and Angela to catch him. He stood swishing his tail as Tim placed the halter over his head. Then they led him over to the gate.

'Phew!' said Duncan.

He and Angela were sweating in the heat.

'We can't do that every time we need to bring him in,' said Angela. 'We'll be exhausted!'

Tim looked worried.

'That's typical for Buttons,' he said. 'It was quite quick compared to how it is usually. Does that mean you won't want him here?'

'Oh no,' said Angela. 'I didn't mean it like that. But I can see it's been hard work for you. And it's a pity you've never had the chance to ride him. Have you ever had any advice on dealing with his behaviour?'

Tim shrugged.

'We've read a few books and tried a couple of different things with him, but nothing seems to have worked. We wanted to talk to the farmer who owned him, to find out more about his background, but he moved abroad and he hasn't returned any of our calls. Maybe he's just a bad pony.'

Tilly felt frustration bubble up inside her.

'There's no such thing as a bad pony,' she said passionately. 'We'll be able to help Buttons, won't we?'

She looked at Angela and Duncan, eyes wide, urging them to agree. Duncan smiled.

'Of course, Tilly,' he said. 'We'll do our best.'

But something in his eyes made Tilly think that he wasn't quite convinced. Nevertheless, she was determined. She wouldn't give up on Buttons, even if everyone else did.

# Three

Next morning, Tilly arrived at Silver
Shoe for her usual round of stable chores:
mucking out, feeding and grooming. The
weather was fine again, so she enjoyed
being in the fresh air. She wore blue
jodhpurs and a red-and-white striped vest
so she could get some sun on her arms.
She wished she didn't have to wear her
riding boots in the heat, but they were
the safest footwear for working around
horses.

Magic was waiting at the stable door. As soon as he saw her, he bobbed his head and pricked his ears.

'Good morning, boy,' she called. 'How are you today?'

She opened the door and gave him a hug.

'Sleep well, did you? Was it a peaceful night?'

Tilly noticed him scraping the floor with his front foot.

'What are you saying?' said Tilly. 'Are you ready for your morning groom?'

He tapped his foot again. Tilly could tell he was keen to get outside.

'Let's get started then,' she said. 'I'll get your food and two buckets of fresh water – it's amazing how much you drink in the hot weather. Then it's grooming time, and after that I'll clean your stable.'

She led Magic into the open and tied him nearby. He stood in the sun, swishing flies with his tail, watching as other horses in the yard were fed and groomed too.

Tim was there, with Buttons. Tilly gave them a wave then fetched two buckets of clean water from the tap.

As she walked back, she noticed Buttons tossing his head. He gave a loud neigh and began to stamp his hooves.

'Hey,' said Tim. 'Calm down, boy!'

He tried to settle Buttons, but Buttons pulled away and continued stamping and neighing. He didn't seem at all keen to be groomed. Soon the noise began to bother the other horses in the yard.

Tilly watched Aladdin, one of the riding school horses, get restless as he was groomed by her friend, Cynthia. Tilly knew Aladdin had a reputation for being feisty, but normally he loved his morning brush.

'Hey! What's got into you?' said Cynthia. 'Easy, boy!'

She gripped his rope tightly. Tilly could tell she was using all her strength to hold him. Eventually he calmed, but Cynthia was clearly shaken.

'Are you okay?' said Tilly.

'Yes, fine. Aladdin's being really boisterous this morning. He doesn't like the fuss that new pony is making.'

'Guinevere is getting annoyed too,' said one of the Silver Shoe regulars. 'She doesn't seem to want to do anything for me this morning. It's not like her.'

Tilly returned to Magic and gave him water and a fresh hay-net, then picked up the shavings fork and began to sift through the bedding. Angela came over. Even she didn't look herself this morning. Her hair was messy and she had dark shadows under her eyes.

'Morning, Tilly,' she said. 'What a night!'

'Looks like you stayed up a bit too late,' said Tilly.

'Was kept up more like. We had trouble with Buttons from dusk till dawn. He was neighing and kicking at his stable door. We tried to move him but he nipped at us whenever we came near. It was so stressful!'

'He's a handful, isn't he?' said Tilly.

'He certainly hasn't had the best of starts here. I hope it's just a case of him being unsettled after the travelling – although it does sound as though he's always been very difficult. We'll do what we can to help . . . '

'We have to try.'

'Of course, but sometimes problems become deeply engrained, Tilly. It's hard to change a pony's ways if he's had them for most of his life. It doesn't help that we

don't know much about his background,
or his life on the farm before Tim and his
mum bought him. And it's such a shame
for Tim, not being able to ride him.'

As Angela said this, Tilly felt a pang
of sadness. It was hard to imagine owning
a horse and never being able to get close
to them.

'I hope there's something we can do,'
she said.

'Me too,' said Angela. 'Between you
and me, I think this is Buttons' last chance.
Tim's mum says if we can't help him to
behave and become ride-worthy, they'll
have to sell him, or worse. It just doesn't
make sense to keep a pony they can't ride.'

'In which case, we definitely have to do
something,' said Tilly. She didn't want to
think about what the 'worse' option might
be.

# Four

That afternoon, Tilly and Mia took their horses, Magic Spirit and Autumn Glory, for a hack. They'd arranged to meet their friend, Cally, and Tilly's brother, Brook, at the gates of Cavendish Hall, the boarding school the two of them attended.

Brook and Tilly had only known each other for a few years, because they'd both been adopted by different families when their birth mum had died. But it was no coincidence that they were horse fanatics.

After finding out their mum had spent time with a horse-loving Native American tribe, they'd guessed it was in their blood. And that's exactly what they talked about as they rode together along the forest track.

'I had an email from Chief Four Paws last night,' said Brook.

Chief Four Paws was the tribe leader. They'd contacted him to see if he knew

anything about their mum and her life. The chief had been very interested in their story, particularly the fact that they'd both been given horsehair bracelets by her, in the same style as his tribe's own bracelets.

'What did he say?' said Tilly excitedly.

'He just asked how we were and how our riding is coming on. He said he's trying to get in contact with some other people

who might remember our mum. As soon as he hears anything he'll let us know.'

'Cool,' said Tilly. She couldn't help being a little disappointed. She was desperate to know more about their connection with the tribe. It was hard having to wait for information.

Just then, a squirrel dropped down from a tree branch and

scampered across their path. It came close to Cally's horse, Mr Fudge, making him spook and leap sideways over a small ditch. He refused to come back over and Cally, clearly shaken, was too nervous to give him a confident kick.

Tilly knew what to do. Without hesitation, she dismounted, passed Magic's reins to Brook, and reached for Mr Fudge's bridle. She held him steady and spoke in a low, firm voice, giving him lots of reassurance. Eventually he relaxed and she led him back onto the path.

'Thanks, Tilly,' said Cally. 'I nearly lost it there! All because of a squirrel! How silly!'

'It could have happened to any of us,' said Tilly.

'It's why we have to keep our wits about us when we're riding,' said Brook. 'You both did well to keep things under control.'

'Mr Fudge did well too,' said Mia, chuckling. 'Squirrels are scary after all!'

Tilly sighed.

'I wish all horses were that easy to manage,' she said. 'There's a pony who's just arrived at Silver Shoe Farm and he's so disobedient. It took Duncan and Angela ages to catch him and bring him in from the field. Then he kicked and neighed all night apparently. And he's never once let his owner ride him. It's got so bad they're thinking of selling him now.'

'Are you talking about the notorious Buttons?' said Mia.

'That's the one.'

'He sounds like hard work,' said Brook. 'Maybe he gets too much attention. The other day I read somewhere that too much petting can lead to naughty behaviour.'

Tilly thought about this. She'd certainly seen Tim be very affectionate towards Buttons. He was often patting and stroking and praising him, even when he was being difficult. Maybe what Buttons really needed was some no-nonsense boundaries?

'Does he have an underlying health problem?' said Cally. 'Sometimes pain can be the cause of a horse's naughtiness. One of the ponies at Cavendish Hall was being a real nightmare, but when he was checked by the dentist they discovered he had a rotten tooth. As soon as it was removed and the pain stopped, he was fine again.'

'The only pain is Buttons himself!' said Mia.

The others laughed.

'Seriously though,' said Tilly. 'These are all good points, but the question is, what can we do to change him?'

When Tilly and Mia got back to Silver Shoe, they discovered things with Buttons had gone from bad to worse. They tied Magic and Autumn Glory in the yard, washed them down, and put them in the paddock to dry off. Then they went straight to the club room for a cool drink. There, they found Duncan, sitting with his leg up on the sofa, holding an ice pack over his knee.

'Oh no,' said Tilly. 'What happened?'

'I was kicked,' said Duncan. 'By our friend Buttons. We were trying to get some tack on him. I don't think he's done any serious damage but I've got a nasty bruise. Lucky he's only 13.2hh. If he'd been any bigger I'd probably have a fractured knee-cap.'

'Ouch!' said Mia.

'Poor you,' said Tilly.

She felt bad for Duncan, but she was also worried this might be the last straw for the little pony. Would Tim and his mum decide to get rid of Buttons now?

'Where is he?'

'He's in the sand school with Angela and Tim. We took him there to help calm him down, and stop him upsetting the other horses. Honestly, I haven't been kicked by a horse in years.'

Tilly could tell it wasn't just Duncan's knee that had been bruised. It was his pride too. She remembered what she'd said to Cally in the woods.

'It could've happened to any of us,' she said. 'At least you were trying to do something to help.'

'Yes, I know,' said Duncan, with a sigh. 'Angela and I were planning to start some lunge work with Buttons, going over the basics to see if that helps. But something tells me it's going to take a lot of time and effort!'

Mia handed Tilly a glass of lemonade.

'Can we get you anything?' she said to Duncan.

'Thanks, girls, but I'm fine. I just need to rest this leg. Why don't you go and see if Tim's all right? He was pretty upset.'

'Come on then,' said Tilly.

# Five

When Tilly and Mia arrived at the sand
school, they saw Angela standing with
Buttons. Tim was watching at the fence.
He looked fed up.

'Hi,' said Tilly. 'I hear Buttons has been
playing up.'

'As usual,' said Tim. He hung his head.
'Is Duncan all right?'

'He'll be fine,' said Mia. 'Don't worry,
Angela and Duncan are the best – they'll
do everything they can to help.'

'I don't know what to do any more.

All I want is to be able to ride Buttons and come hacking with you guys. Is it really too much to ask? We get on fine when we're together, but as soon as I try and put some tack on him, he goes nuts!'

'My brother, Brook, had an idea,' said Tilly. 'He said that sometimes too much petting can make a horse misbehave. Maybe you could try being a bit firmer with him.'

Tim shrugged.

'I don't want to be his enemy,' he said. 'Things are already bad enough.'

'I know what you mean,' said Tilly. 'But it's not about being enemies. It's about letting him know who's boss. Duncan thought going back to basics and doing lots of lunge exercises might help.'

The three of them stared across the sand school. Angela had finally managed to get Buttons to stand still. She led him towards the entrance gate and gave Tim a wave. 'Why don't you put him in the orchard, next to Lulabelle in the small field?' she suggested. 'I don't want them in a field together in case he goes for her, but Lulabelle is a mature, gentle mare. She won't cause him any bother.'

'Okay,' said Tim.

He took the lead rein from Angela. As he walked away, Jack Fisher came by.

'Hello, everyone!'

'Hi, Dad!' said Angela. She greeted him with a big hug. 'You're back. How was your holiday?'

'Oh, it was lovely. I'd forgotten how much I enjoy carriage driving. Doug and Sue are really into it, they even enter roadster competitions sometimes. Got me thinking. I've missed this place though. Who's that then?'

He nodded towards the back-view of Buttons, twitching ears, tail swishing.

'That's our latest guest,' said Angela. 'One to watch, I'm afraid. He's a tricky little pony who doesn't want to be ridden. We're going to start doing some lunging and long-reining. Maybe you could take a look at him and give us your expert opinion?'

While Mia went back to the yard to check on Magic and Autumn Glory, Tilly caught up with Tim and they walked together down to the orchard. It didn't get used very often because the grass wasn't as good as in the other fields.

'Here we are,' said Tilly. 'This is the gate. Hi, Belle.'

Tilly reached a hand across the fence and Lulabelle came towards her. She nuzzled Tilly's arm for a moment, then caught sight of Buttons. She looked at him and nickered. Buttons tossed his head and shuffled away, ears pinned back. He obviously wasn't in a friendly mood.

Tilly opened the gate and Tim tried to lead him in. He tickled his nose and gave him lots of encouragement. Buttons wouldn't go through the gate. Tim spent a few more minutes petting and asking, but Buttons still refused.

'Let me try,' said Tilly.

She took the rein from Tim and held out her hand so Buttons could get used to her scent. Normally she was very quiet and gentle around the horses she was getting to know. This time she knew she had to assert herself.

'Hello, you. Mr Big Stuff, eh?' she said sternly. 'Well, I'm Tilly and I'm not going to take any of your nonsense.'

Buttons pulled his head away. Tilly held the lead rein firmly in place, making it hard for him to move far.

'Don't try any of that with me,' she said. 'We're going into this field and we're going to be very nice to our friend, Lulabelle, who's just next door. Walk on.'

Tilly clicked a couple of times, then gave a sharp tug on the rope and clicked again. Buttons followed. He walked with her to the middle of the field, where they stopped.

'Good boy,' she said approvingly. 'That's much better.'

She tickled his ears and stroked his nose. He seemed to enjoy the attention and lowered his head for more.

'Now, let's go over and say hi to Lulabelle, shall we? I'm sure she'd like to meet you properly.'

Tilly gave Buttons a firm signal to walk on and he followed her to the fence. Lulabelle came forward to greet him, but he snorted and pulled back his ears.

'No,' said Tilly, tugging his halter. 'Lulabelle is a friend. We mustn't be mean to our friends.'

Buttons snorted again, but he relaxed his ears. He lowered his head as though he was asking for more attention.

'Show me how you behave nicely first,' said Tilly. 'Then you can have your tickles.'

When she could see he was relaxed, she led him back towards Lulabelle. Lulabelle bobbed her head and this time

Buttons stood calmly. He didn't make any friendly advances towards her but he didn't make any unfriendly ones either.

'Well done, boy!' said Tilly, patting him affectionately.

'I can't believe it,' said Tim, as they walked back through the gate and left Buttons to settle. 'The way he was with you. He really cooperated. He must like you. Mia was right – you've obviously got a natural way with horses.'

Tilly smiled.

'It's like I said, maybe we need to be strict with him and save the petting for rewards and special occasions.'

Tim nodded and looked hopeful.

'Thanks,' he said. 'I see what you mean now.'

# Six

Over the next few weeks Tilly was busy
with end of term activities. She only
managed to spend a little time each
morning and evening at Silver Shoe, so the
following Thursday when school finally
broke up for the summer, she was eager
to spend the rest of the day there. And
the next day. And the day after that.

'I love the summer holidays,' she said, as
she prepared a sandwich in the club room to
fuel herself for an afternoon of stable work.
'It means I get to be here all the time.'

'I'm sure you'll make the most of it,' said Angela.

Angela was tidying the club room notice-board. She took down the out-of-date adverts about second-hand trailers, tack and riding boots, and put up new ones.

'How's Buttons getting on?'

'Hmm,' said Angela. She stopped what she was doing and turned to Tilly. 'I'd like to say we've worked a miracle, but unfortunately progress is slow. We've done lots of lunging this week and he's starting to focus. Trouble is, with the yard so full at the moment, Duncan and I haven't got much time to spare. I don't think Tim will be riding Buttons any time soon.'

'At least Buttons has responded,' said Tilly. 'There's hope. I was worried that no one would be able to do anything.'

'Yes,' said Angela. 'I suppose that's something.'

'Maybe I could help?' she said brightly. 'Now I'm on holiday I've got plenty of time.'

Angela thought for a minute.

'Actually, that would be great. I'm sure Tim would appreciate it. Although you have to remember, Tilly, Buttons is quite a character. You'll need to be very firm with him. I know you've had experience helping with nervy, scared or even mischievous horses, and you've worked wonders with Magic, but Buttons is an extreme case. He's super smart. And he's easily bored, so you have to keep challenging him.'

'I can do that,' said Tilly.

'I know you can,' said Angela, with a smile.

Tilly didn't waste any time. She found Tim sitting on a bench in the yard, reading a horse magazine.

'Hey, how are you?' she said, flopping down beside him.

'Oh, hi, Tilly.'

'What are you up to? I haven't read that magazine yet. Is there anything good in it?'

'I was just browsing the pony-for-sale adverts. Mia said you guys used them when you were trying to find her a new horse. Maybe there's a pony for me in here somewhere? What about this one: chestnut, 13hh, well-disciplined riding school pony, needs good home?'

'I didn't know you were looking for another pony,' said Tilly.

'Well, I can't help wondering if it's time to give up on Buttons. When I see you and Mia going riding every day with Magic and Autumn, I feel as though I'm really missing out. I want to be able to *do* something with my pony, not just stare at him in a field. My mum's running out of patience and I'm starting to as well.

She suggested we put an advert out in the next few days, to see if we can sell him on. After all, he's been here for nearly two weeks and he's hardly shown any improvement.'

'But he has. He has started to improve!'

'I still haven't been able to ride him, though, have I?'

Tilly sighed and clenched her fists.

'Please,' she said. 'Don't give up just yet. Put that magazine away and come with me. We're going to try a few things first.'

'What do you mean?'

Tilly explained that Angela had asked her to help with the lunging.

'There's no time like the present,' she said. 'Let's get to work.'

They found Duncan, who agreed to supervise, then they went to the tack room to collect a lunge rope and whip.

It had been a while since Tilly had done anything like this. She remembered how she'd helped Duncan when they were first training Magic. Magic had been stubborn, but every time Tilly had taken the reins, he'd cooperated. If she could do it with Magic, maybe she'd be able to do it with Buttons too.

As they crossed the yard, they saw Jack Fisher. Tilly held up the ropes.

'We're going to try working with Buttons,' she told him.

'If you think you can do something,' said Jack, 'go for it, but I'm not sure that pony's for riding. I'll come down later and see how you're getting on. I'm reading up on carriage driving – nothing like a holiday for rediscovering old hobbies.' He waved a dusty-looking book at her.

Tilly was surprised. She wasn't sure what he meant about Buttons not being for riding. It wasn't like Jack to be so negative about a horse or pony. She wasn't going to let him put her off.

Buttons was in the orchard. To Tilly's delight, when she called his name he pricked his ears and came straight to the fence. He hadn't done that with anyone else, apart from Tim.

'Hello, boy,' said Tim. Buttons lowered his head and Tim allowed him to explore the feel and smell of his hands. On Tilly's advice, he didn't overdo it. He petted him briefly then showed him the lunge rope. Buttons nudged it with his nose.

It was clear to Tilly that, despite everything, the bond between them was strong. It seemed such a shame that they were considering selling him. What would happen to the little pony then?

'That's it, Buttons,' she said encouragingly. 'How do you fancy doing some work with us? We'll take you back to the yard, give you a quick groom, then go over to the sand school. We'll have plenty of room there.'

Tim held the head collar and lead rope behind his back with one hand, then approached Buttons from the side with a bucket of nuts in his other hand. Buttons put his nose straight into the bucket. He flinched for a second, then allowed Tim to slip the head collar over his head. Tim couldn't believe it.

'That was the easiest it's ever been!'

Together, Tim and Tilly gave Buttons a thorough groom. He seemed to relish all the fuss and attention – it was so different to how he'd been when he'd first arrived, neighing and stamping his hooves. He clearly had things he liked and didn't like. He enjoyed having his whole body brushed but he wasn't so keen on having anything near his face. Tilly kept this to a minimum, just a quick wipe with a damp sponge.

'There you go. Much fresher,' she said. 'Now, let me give your tail a quick comb.'

She ran the comb through his grey tail hairs and gathered up the loose ones. She didn't say anything to Tim, but she hoped she could give him a bracelet on the day he had his first ride. She glanced at the lunge rope, which was hanging over a nearby fencepost, then back at Buttons. With any luck, that would be soon.

# Seven

Buttons walked alongside Tilly and Tim towards the sand school where Duncan was waiting. He needed the occasional pull and click to remind him to stay at Tilly's side, not to dawdle or to go too far ahead. Tilly remembered what Angela had said about being strong. She was glad Buttons wanted to cooperate today, but she knew she couldn't let it go to her head. They had to show him who was boss.

They reached the gate. Tim opened it and Tilly led Buttons inside. Duncan had recently harrowed the surface so the footing was perfect. Tilly prepared the lunge rein. She folded it back and forth on itself, taking care to see there were no twists or knots. She attached the end of the rope to the bottom ring of Button's halter and stepped back, creating a good five metre stretch between them.

Duncan checked she'd done it properly.

'Looks good,' he said. 'Now we're ready.'

Duncan demonstrated some warm-up exercises, getting Buttons to walk in small and large circles, and in different directions. Then he asked Tilly to take over.

Suddenly, Tilly's mouth went dry with nerves. She felt conscious of everything – the heat of the sun, the tension in her legs, the fact that Tim and Duncan were watching, or that anyone walking past would be able to see what she was doing, and see whether she was making a mess of things or not. She wanted to get this right, for Buttons' sake and Tim's.

'Remember to keep a triangle, between horse, lunge rein and whip,' said Duncan.

Tilly took a deep breath, checked her position and prepared for the first command. With a flick of the lunge whip and a firm voice, she asked Buttons to walk on. He stood quietly, as though he hadn't heard her. She waited a moment, then repeated the command. Still, he didn't move.

'Please,' she said, giving a double click.

Buttons snorted and responded to the command.

Tilly beckoned Tim over.

'Here,' she said, handing him the whip and rope. 'Something tells me you should have a go with him.'

'Me?' said Tim.

'Go for it,' she said. 'Be firm. He seems to respond well to that double-click.'

Tim took Tilly's place, and repeated the command. This time, Buttons did as he was told. Tilly and Duncan smiled and nodded at each other.

'That must feel good for both of them,' whispered Duncan.

Tilly agreed. It was great to see them working together. Tim looked as though he was concentrating hard, but he was completely in control.

'Well done!' he said. 'Now, let's try a trot. Okay. Terr-ott!' He made a double-clicking noise too.

Immediately, and without needing a prompt from the whip this time, Buttons picked up the pace and moved into an elegant trot. He completed a couple of circles then came to a halt when he was asked to.

'That was perfect,' said Duncan. 'Well done, guys! And that was good instinct on your part, Tilly – you could see that Buttons wanted to work with Tim. He's a capable little pony, so it still puzzles me that he refuses to be ridden. But we'll get to that point eventually. Right, back to it. Do you want another go, Tilly?'

'Okay,' she said. 'I hope he performs for me. We'll try a trot to canter, then canter to trot.'

Tim gave her the lunge rope and whip.

To Tilly's relief, when she gave the command, Buttons obliged. He did a smooth transition into an even canter.

He didn't once become too strong or lose balance, and he kept rhythm the whole time. It looked amazing. Tilly imagined for a second that she was a Native American tribe member, working with a wild Mustang. She thought Chief Four Paws would be proud of her.

As Tilly was slowing Buttons to a trot, Jack Fisher appeared.

'My word!' he said. He took his cap off and stood watching. 'You have managed to make progress!'

Tilly could tell he was impressed. She carried on with what she was doing.

'Keep focused,' she murmured to herself.

Eventually she asked Buttons to come back into a walk, and then asked him to halt. When they were done, Jack clapped.

'I've said it before and I'll say it again. Tilly, you're a natural. You've got a gift. And as for you, Buttons, maybe you aren't such a tricky one after all.'

Tilly grinned from ear-to-ear. She was pleased to be given a compliment, but most of all, she was happy for Tim and Buttons. At last, things were starting to look up.

# Eight

For the rest of the week, Tilly and Tim tried different long-reining exercises with Buttons. It seemed to be going well, and Buttons even let them put some tack on him, although Tim hadn't tried riding him again yet. Of course Tilly also had her usual work around the farm to do as well – mucking out, sweeping the yard, helping move horses from field to field, grooming, feeding and exercising Magic – but she didn't mind being busy. She was glad to spend the long school-free days doing what she liked best. And she was keeping her fingers crossed that Tim had forgotten all about wanting to sell Buttons.

On Friday afternoon, the sand school was being used for lessons, so Tilly and Tim decided to continue their work with Buttons in the orchard. Tilly put Magic in the next field so that he could watch what they were doing. He stood at the fence the whole time. Tilly knew he wanted to be close to her, so she made sure she gave him lots of attention, calling back and explaining what she was doing with Buttons.

'We're going to try steering in and out of cones today, then stopping at the marker. Remember when I long-reined you, Magic? It seems like such a long time ago now. Look how far you've come!'

Magic bobbed his head. Buttons shuffled his hooves. Tilly thought he might be a bit put off by Magic's presence.

'You'll have to get used to it, Buttons,' she said firmly. 'There are other horses and ponies in the world besides you, you know.'

He shook his head and snorted.

'Come on. Don't get grumpy with us now.'

Tim patted his neck and showed him the lunge ropes. They didn't need to use the whip as much any more because Buttons was responding quickly to their voice aids. They did some normal lunging so that the commands were fresh in Buttons' mind, then Tilly added a second lunge rope. She fed them both through the stirrups and clipped them to his bit.

'Ready, then.'

Tim got himself into position behind, very slightly to one side, so Buttons could still see him. Tilly stood nearby, ready to make suggestions.

'Walk on,' said Tim.

Buttons did as he was told. They made it to the other end of the field then halted, steered and turned.

'You're driving him. Excellent,' said Tilly. 'You're doing great! Now let's try it with some cones. I saw this on a Youtube clip.'

Tim walked Buttons forward. Slowly he navigated his way around them. He knocked one aside, but cleared the others. He seemed really comfortable with the feel of long-reining, as though he'd done it before. When they tried it a second time, they were even more successful – no cones down.

After twenty minutes they stopped for a rest. Tim gave Buttons a rewarding pat, then let him graze for a bit, while Tilly

fussed over Magic. She stroked his neck and gave him a kiss on the nose. When Buttons wasn't looking she slipped him one of his favourite treats, a mint.

'Good boy, you're being really patient. We'll go hacking later, I promise.'

Moments later Mia and Duncan came by.

'Hey, guys,' said Mia. 'I thought we'd find you both here. How's it going?'

'Seems to be looking good,' said Duncan. 'Lots of people around the farm have commented that Buttons seems much calmer. It's down to you two and your hard work. Well done.'

'Thanks,' said Tim. 'Maybe I could try riding him today? What do you think? How's your knee?'

'It's much better,' said Duncan. 'No harm done. Oh! Look at that!'

They turned to see Buttons and Magic sniffing each other at the fence. While Tilly, Mia, Tim and Duncan were talking, Buttons had wandered over.

Amazingly, he was being friendly. His ears were pricked forwards instead of back. There was no sign of aggression or hostility.

'Now, that is progress!' said Duncan. 'Every time we've tried to put him near other horses he's nipped them.'

'He wouldn't dare bite Magic, would you, Buttons?'

She patted his neck and ran her fingers through his mane.

'So, do you think he *is* ready for Tim to ride?' she said.

'Well, we can try,' said Duncan. 'Angela is finished in the sand school now so let's see what we can do.'

# Nine

'Today's the day!' said Tim. 'I can feel it!'

Tilly could hear the excitement in his voice.

'Hopefully,' said Tilly. 'He seems really relaxed.'

Tim crossed his fingers.

'Please. Please. Please. All this time I've kept him and not been able to ride him – I can't wait!'

They returned to the yard to find Buttons and Duncan waiting with Mia. Jack Fisher had joined them and was keen to see how things would work out.

'So, you're going to try a ride?' he said to Tim.

Tim nodded and gave Buttons a pat on the shoulder.

'Okay.'

Jack gave an odd smile and folded his arms.

'I still wonder about Buttons,' he said. 'But let's see what happens.'

Tilly was puzzled. What did Jack mean? She was disappointed he seemed so doubtful after all the hard work they'd put in. She hoped for Tim's sake that he'd be proved wrong.

Tim gave Tilly a big grin. She crossed her fingers.

They held Buttons steady while Duncan checked all his tack. Buttons had got used to wearing it while they had been long-reining him, but Duncan wanted to be sure everything was just right. He lengthened the stirrups and tightened the girth. Buttons seemed a little nervous but he didn't make a fuss. Then they led him down to the sand school.

Tilly passed Tim his riding hat.

'Good luck,' she whispered.

Duncan held Buttons' reins, Tim came round to his side and prepared to mount. Buttons stood still. Tim placed his left hand on the saddle and got his foot into the stirrup. It was all looking good and then – it all went wrong! Just as Tim tried to swing his leg over, Buttons pulled away. He was so strong that even Duncan couldn't hold him, and Tim hopped and wobbled behind, and fell in a heap on the floor.

Buttons neighed loudly. It was obvious he wasn't going to let Tim ride him. Tilly's spirits sank. She wished she could explain to Buttons how important it was, how much Tim wanted to ride him, and how close he was to being sold.

'It's his last chance,' she said to Mia quietly. 'I wish he'd understand that.'

Mia shook her head with frustration.

'I feel sorry for both of them,' she said.

Tim clenched his fists and sighed.

'I got so close,' he said. 'He nearly let me.'

'Let's not give up just yet,' said Duncan.

'Why?' said Jack bluntly. 'I'm just not convinced that pony is for riding. Sorry, Tim, that's how it is. But I've been doing a bit of reading, and I may have an idea that'll work.'

'What's that?' said Duncan.

'I've been watching Buttons, the way he moves and holds his neck, the way he's responded to the long-reining exercises. He reminds of an old Cyldie we used to have, who was a great carriage horse. It made me think we should give Buttons a try with a trap or a small cart. In fact, I'd bet money he's been used as a driving pony in the past.'

Tim and Tilly looked at each other and shrugged. It had never crossed Tilly's mind before, but she liked the idea. Tim did too.

'I'll try anything,' he said.

Duncan gave a nod.

'It's worth a go,' he said, with a grin. 'I know Angela keeps a driving cart in one of the old sheds. Let's give it a try.'

With renewed enthusiasm, Tilly and Tim kept Buttons company, while Duncan and Jack went to fetch the cart.

'I can't wait to see this,' said Tilly. 'Jack knows loads about horses. His instincts are always good.'

'I hope so,' said Tim. 'It makes sense, what he says. We never really knew what Buttons did before we got him. We just assumed he was used for riding, but maybe he pulled a trap around the farm.'

Duncan and Jack got the little cart out of the shed and brought it over to one of the flat paddocks, where Angela joined them and helped to wipe it down.

It was in decent condition. It just needed a clean. As soon as Buttons saw it, he wanted to go over.

'That's a good sign,' said Tilly.

'I'm pleased this old thing is going to get put to use,' said Angela. 'Let's go and get the right tack.'

Tim held on to Buttons, who was able to watch the preparation of the cart, while Tilly and Angela went to the tack room. They hunted through all the bridles and bits, until they found a special one used for driving. Angela also found a breast collar harness which was to be attached to the trap. She checked it over to make sure it wasn't damaged in any way.

'He can use this stuff for now,' she said, as they rejoined the others in the paddock. 'But, who knows, if he takes to it, maybe one day he'll have his own tack, made-to-measure?'

'Maybe,' said Tim. Tilly could see he wasn't quite sure what to expect. She crossed her fingers for the second time that day.

# Ten

Buttons allowed Angela to tack him up with the driving bridle and collar harness. When Duncan and Jack put him to the little cart he instinctively wanted to pull it forward. Tim and Tilly and Mia stood watching.

'The collar will place the weight of the load on to his sternum,' Jack explained, as he checked all the straps. 'It's only a light vehicle so it won't restrict his air supply. When driving a cart, it's really important to look at everything thoroughly before you get on. Make sure none of the straps are twisted and everything's buckled. There are lots of parts to a harness and they all need to be secure.'

'Right,' said Duncan. 'We're ready.'

'I think it's best if I drive first,' said Jack. 'Since I'm the only person who's had any experience with a pony and trap. Then maybe, Tim, you can have a go.'

'Er, okay,' said Tim hesitantly. He looked at Tilly. 'It's nothing like riding, is it? I'm not sure I'll be any good.'

'Just give it a try,' said Tilly. 'You might love it.'

'Buttons certainly seems to – look at him!'

Buttons ears were pricked forward and he was the calmest they'd ever seen him. As the cart pulled away with Jack Fisher on board, he was focused and keen. They went in a straight line across the paddock. Tim gasped. He couldn't believe it.

'It's like watching a different pony. Jack was right.'

'Jack's always right,' said Duncan, with a grin.

'Right, Tim,' said Jack, pulling to a halt in front of them. 'Now it's your turn. Don't worry, I'll be sitting next to you the whole time, I'll just let you take the reins for a couple of minutes and show you how.'

Before getting into the cart, Tim went round to the front and gave Buttons a long cuddle.

'Wow! You were so impressive, boy!' Tilly heard him whisper. 'I didn't know you had it in you.'

Buttons lowered his head and Tim tickled his ears. He went round to the side of the cart and, with Duncan's help, climbed on.

'Will he be able to pull both of us?' asked Tim, looking a bit concerned.

'Ponies are stronger than you think,' said Jack. 'And don't forget he's pulling us rather than carrying us. We'll only do it for a few minutes. You'll need to have proper lessons before you can ride in the cart on your own,' he explained.

As Tilly watched, she remembered the hairs she'd collected from Button's tail. They were still in her pocket. She took them out and began to plait them – it seemed like the perfect time to give a bracelet to Tim. He was riding Buttons for the first time, even if it wasn't the kind of ride he'd been expecting.

'Pick up the reins and don't let go of them,' said Jack. 'Buttons is already flicking back his ears, listening out for what you want him to do. He really gets this.

Do you feel comfortable?'

'Yes,' said Tim. He gave Tilly and Mia a wave. 'Actually, it feels great!'

'Take the whip in your right hand. You may not have to use it if he responds to your voice. Draw the reins up so you have gentle contact with his mouth. Sit up straight, brace your feet against the base of the cart, and when you're ready, ask him to walk on.'

Tim adjusted his position slightly. He gave a nervous smile then looked ahead.

'Walk on!' he said, and immediately the cart rumbled forward. Within moments, the pair of them seemed perfectly settled into their roles. They got to the fence then turned and did two more laps. They even managed to work up to a trot.

'It's as if you've been driving together for years,' said Jack. 'I'm almost as impressed with you as I am with Buttons.'

Tilly and Mia applauded.

After two laps of trotting, the cart slowed down again, and with Jack's encouragement, Tim attempted to steer Buttons in a figure-of-eight formation. It was nearly exact. He picked up the pace, did several more laps of fast trot, and came to a halt.

'I can't believe how much fun this is!' said Tim. 'I wish I'd tried it years ago.'

'I think Buttons would agree with you,' said Angela.

Buttons gave a little snort.

'You look fantastic up there,' said Duncan. 'You've taken to it really quickly.'

'You should get involved in competitions – the folks over at Cavendish Hall are organising a roadster event at the end of the summer. Maybe you and Buttons could start training for it?' said Jack.

'Wow! Maybe we will. Thanks, everyone,' said Tim. 'Without you, we would never have been able to do this, and I'd never have known what a brilliant pony Buttons really is.'

He looked at Tilly.

'And thanks to you especially. I know how much time you've spent working with Buttons. Everyone says you've got a magic touch when it comes to horses and ponies. And I know what they mean. You're amazing.'

Tilly blushed and smiled.

'Hey, do you want a ride?'

'I'd love one,' said Tilly. 'Would that be okay?'

'Come on then!' said Jack. He took the reins from Tim, and Tim got out to make space for Tilly.

Tilly had never sat in a cart or carriage before. It felt strange but good.

'Why don't you give the command this time?' Jack suggested.

'Come on then, Buttons. Walk on! *Click-click*,' she said firmly.

As they moved off she was certain Buttons recognised her voice.

He looked round and gave a nod, as though he was letting them know he approved of his new passenger. They did a few circuits of the paddock and then Jack gave Tilly the reins. Finally, they came to a stop.

'It's cool, isn't it?' said Tim, coming over to them. 'Different to riding, but I like the way it feels. And Buttons loves it. He hasn't needed the whip once. I didn't realise he could be this obedient. I can't wait to learn how to do it properly and go out on my own, around the farm, out on the road, maybe even enter competitions!'

'So you won't be selling Buttons after all?'

Tim looked at Tilly. There was a twinkle in his eye.

'No way.'

'Which means I should definitely give you this,' she said, reaching into her pocket. She handed Tim the bracelet she'd made.

'Oh,' he said. 'It's like the ones you wear.'

'Except this one is made from Buttons' tail-hairs, so it's special to you.'

'Thanks, Tilly,' he said. 'Can you tie it on?'

He held out his arm and Tilly fastened the bracelet around his wrist. They grinned at one another.

'Can I have one more lap?' asked Tim.

'Why not?' said Tilly, jumping out so that Tim could climb in again. 'What do you think, Buttons?'

Buttons pricked his ears. Watching them pull away, Tilly sighed happily. She hadn't been certain that things would work out between Tim and Buttons, but now it was clear they were on the right track. Tilly hoped the pair of them would stay at Silver Shoe for a long time. She was looking forward to many future cart rides with her two new friends.

# Pippa's Top Tips

Bridles and saddles used every day need to be cleaned and looked after properly and checked regularly. Pay attention to the stitching – if this begins to go it could be dangerous.

Tack is expensive – the better it's cared for, the longer it will last.

If your pony is naughty to catch, take a bucket of food with you and leave a head collar on. Never try to chase them, you are better off standing still or quietly walking towards them.

Concentrate at all times when out riding because you can never predict what is around the corner.

Sometimes, giving your horse too much attention can lead to naughty behaviour. Be firm – it's not about being enemies, but you need to let him know who's boss.

If your horse or pony is naughty, it could be because of an underlying health problem. Check with your vet if you're not sure.

When leading your pony you should always try to stay level with his shoulder. It is the safest place to be and you have more strength to control him from there.

Always lead your pony from his left side, so that your right side is his left, and turn him away from you so that you are on his outside as he turns.

Long-reining and lunge exercises are a good way of going back to basics with a pony who doesn't want to be ridden. But never do anything without an experienced adult who knows what they are doing, because it can be dangerous.

Ponies are stronger than you think, especially when they are pulling a cart rather than carrying a rider.

# Glossary

**Halter / head collar (p.10)** – This is used to lead a horse or pony, or tie it up, and usually made of leather or webbing.

**Girth (p.10)** – Leather or webbing strap which passes under the horse's stomach and is attached on both sides of the saddle to hold it in place.

**Hacking (p.21)** – Riding in the country for pleasure.

**Mucking out (p.29)** – Your horse or pony's stable needs mucking out once or twice a day, to remove droppings and wet bedding and then replace with fresh bedding.

**Grooming (p.29)** – Regular grooming cleans your horse and will prevent any chafing under tack. It keeps your horse healthy and comfortable and will help you form a relationship with him.

**hh / hands high (p.42)** – Horses and ponies are measured in 'hands', a hand is 4 inches or 10.16 cm.

**Lunging (p.44)** – Guiding a horse forward and using your voice to ask him to walk, trot and canter. You stand in the middle and he circles around you on the end of a long rope or lunge line.

**Roadster competition (p.48)** – A type of competition where horses or ponies are hitched to light carts which they pull around an arena. They are tested on performance and manners.

**Carriage horse (p.81)** – A horse which pulls traps, wagons or carts.

**Bit (p.83)** – Part of the bridle that sits in your horse or pony's mouth. It is normally made of metal but there are also synthetic types which are made of rubber, for example. There are many different types of bit – all of which have different effects.

# Points of a Horse

1. poll
2. ear
3. eye
4. mane
5. crest
6. withers
7. back
8. loins
9. croup
10. dock
11. flank
12. tail
13. tendons
14. hock joint
15. stomach
16. elbow
17. heel
18. hoof
19. coronet band
20. pastern
21. fetlock joint
22. cannon bone
23. knee
24. shoulder
25. chin groove
26. nostril
27. muzzle
28. nose
29. cheekbone
30. forelock

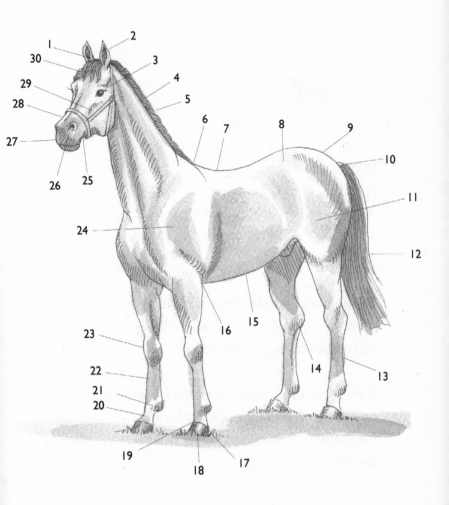

# Pippa Funnell

*"Winning is amazing for a minute, but then I am striving again to reach my next goal."*

I began learning to ride when I was six, on a little pony called Pepsi.

When I was seven, I joined my local Pony Club – the perfect place to learn more about riding and caring for horses.

By the time I was fourteen and riding my first horse, Sir Barnaby, my dream of being an event rider was starting to take shape.

Two years later, I was offered the opportunity to train as a working pupil in Norfolk with Ruth McMullen, the legendary riding teacher. I jumped at the chance.

In 1987, Sir Barnaby and I won the individual gold together at the Young Rider European Championships, which was held in Poland.

Since then, hard work and determination have taken me all the way to the biggest eventing competitions in the world. I've been lucky and had success at major events like Bramham, Burghley, Badminton, Luhmühlen, Le Lion d'Angers, Hickstead, Blenheim, Windsor, Saumur, Pau, Kentucky – and the list goes on…

I married William Funnell in 1993. William is an international show jumper and horse breeder. He has helped me enormously with my show jumping. We live on a farm in the beautiful Surrey countryside – with lots of stables!

Every sportsman or woman's wildest dream is to be asked to represent their country at the Olympics. So in 2000, when I was chosen for the Sydney Olympics, I was delighted. It was even more special to be part of the silver medal winning team.

Then, in 2003, I became the first (and only) person to win eventing's most coveted prize – the Rolex Grand Slam. The Grand Slam (winning three of the big events in a row – Badminton, Kentucky and Burghley) is the only three-day eventing slam in the sporting world.

2004 saw another Olympics and another call-up. Team GB performed brilliantly again and won another well-deserved silver medal, and I was lucky enough to win an individual bronze.

Having had several years without any top horses, I spent my time producing youngsters, so it was great in 2010 when one of those came through – Redesigned, a handsome chestnut gelding. In June that year I won my third Bramham International Horse Trials title on Redesigned. We even managed a clear show jumping round in the pouring rain! By the end of 2010, Redesigned was on the squad for the World Championships in Kentucky where we finished fifth.

Today, as well as a hectic competition schedule, I'm also busy training horses for the future. At the Billy Stud, I work with my husband, William, and top breeder, Donal Barnwell, to produce top-class sport horses.

And in between all that I love writing the *Tilly's Pony Tails* books, and I'm also a trustee of World Horse Welfare, a fantastic charity dedicated to giving abused and neglected horses a second chance in life. For more information, visit their website at www.worldhorsewelfare.org.

# Acknowledgements

Three years ago when my autobiography was published I never imagined that I would find myself writing children's books. Huge thanks go to Louisa Leaman for helping me to bring Tilly to life, and to Jennifer Miles for her wonderful illustrations.

Many thanks to Fiona Kennedy for persuading and encouraging me to search my imagination and for all her hard work, along with the rest of the team at Orion. Due to my riding commitments I am not the easiest person to get hold of as my agent Jonathan Marks at MTC has found. It's a relief he has been able to work on all the agreements for me.

Much of my thinking about Tilly has been done out loud in front of family, friends and godchildren – thank you all for listening.

More than anything I have to acknowledge my four-legged friends – my horses. It is thanks to them, and the great moments I have had with them, that I was able to create a girl, Tilly, who like me follows her passions.

Pippa Funnell
Forest Green, February 2009

For more about Tilly and
Silver Shoe Farm – including pony tips,
quizzes and everything you ever wanted
to know about horses –
visit www.tillysponytails.co.uk